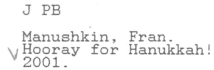

For Jake Levin
—F.M.

For my cousins Molly and Zachary Rosen with love and latkes
—C.C.

Text copyright © 2001 by Fran Manushkin. Illustrations copyright © 2001 by Carolyn Croll.
All rights reserved under International and Pan-American Copyright Conventions.
Published in the United States by Random House, Inc., New York, and simultaneously
in Canada by Random House of Canada Limited, Toronto.

www.randomhouse.com/kids

Library of Congress Cataloging-in-Publication Data
Manushkin, Fran.   Hooray for Hanukkah! / by Fran Manushkin.   p.   cm.
SUMMARY: A menorah describes a family's joyous celebration of this
Jewish holiday, from the first night to the eighth and last.
ISBN 0-375-81043-9 (trade) — ISBN 0-375-91043-3 (lib. bdg.)
[1. Hanukkah—Fiction.   2. Jews—United States—Fiction.]
I. Title.   PZ7.M3195 Hu   2001   [E]—dc21   00-055302
Printed in the United States of America   August 2001   10 9 8 7 6 5 4 3 2 1

Hooray for Hanukkah!

By Fran Manushkin
Illustrated by Carolyn Croll

Random House 🏠 New York

Hooray for Hanukkah! It's my favorite holiday. I'll tell you why. I am a menorah!

In winter, when it's cold and dark, my colorful candles are warm and bright. Hooray! Hooray for Hanukkah!

Hanukkah lasts for eight happy days.
On the first night, Mama says the blessings
and lights the first candle. She uses a helper
candle called the shammas.

Friends see me in the window and
they come to visit. See how I glow?
I am bright, but I *could* be brighter.

On the second night, the family lights TWO candles.
They gather around and sing to me, *"Oh, Hanukkah!*
Oh, Hanukkah! Come light the menorah!"
My TWO candles sparkle and glow.
I am bright, but I *could* be brighter.

On the third night, Grandma
lights THREE candles.

The family makes potato pancakes called latkes.

The latkes are as golden as my flames.
My THREE candles sparkle and glow.
I am bright, but I *could* be brighter.

On the fourth night, Grandpa lights FOUR candles. He teaches the children how to play dreidel. They spin the dreidel and win prizes. The kitten spins it, too!

I see my flames shining in the kitten's eyes.
My FOUR candles glimmer and glow.
I am bright, but I *could* be brighter.

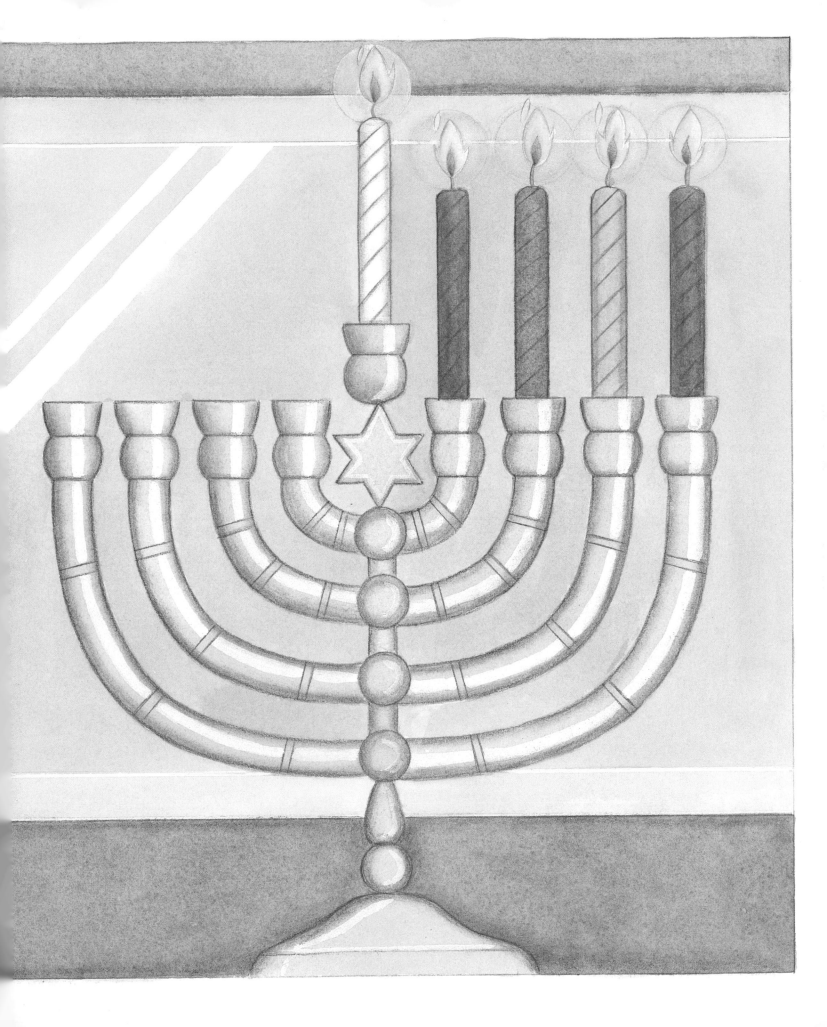

On the fifth night, the children light FIVE candles.
Mama gives them Hanukkah money. The coins are gold,
but inside, there is chocolate!

Hanukkah is a sweet holiday.
My FIVE candles light up the children's
happy, sticky faces.
I am bright, but I *could* be brighter.

On the sixth night, Papa lights SIX candles. He leads the family in a noisy dance around and around me!

My flames dance, too! See them sway and reach up, UP, UP!

I am bright, but I *could* be brighter.

On the seventh night, it snows!
The children light SEVEN candles.
My flames glow in the window, lighting the way to our house. Our friends can find us in the snow. Here come more gifts and kisses and hugs.

I am bright, but I *could* be brighter.

Finally, here it is: the eighth night of Hanukkah.

The family gathers around me, and each person lights a candle. They light one, two, three, four, five, six, seven, EIGHT candles!

Mama turns out the lights, and everyone says *Ooh!* and *Aah!*

I am the brightest I can be! My brave light pushes the darkness away. That's what Hanukkah is all about.

All year long, the family will remember my eight bright days.

That's why everyone says, "Hooray! Hooray for Hanukkah!"